Dear Parents:

Congratulations! Your child is taking the first steps on an exciting journey. The destination? Independent reading!

STEP INTO READING® will help your child get there. The program offers five steps to reading success. Each step includes fun stories and colorful art or photographs. In addition to original fiction and books with favorite characters, there are Step into Reading Non-Fiction Readers, Phonics Readers and Boxed Sets, Sticker Readers, and Comic Readers—a complete literacy program with something to interest every child.

Learning to Read, Step by Step!

Ready to Read **Preschool–Kindergarten**
• big type and easy words • rhyme and rhythm • picture clues
For children who know the alphabet and are eager to begin reading.

Reading with Help **Preschool–Grade 1**
• basic vocabulary • short sentences • simple stories
For children who recognize familiar words and sound out new words with help.

Reading on Your Own **Grades 1–3**
• engaging characters • easy-to-follow plots • popular topics
For children who are ready to read on their own.

Reading Paragraphs **Grades 2–3**
• challenging vocabulary • short paragraphs • exciting stories
For newly independent readers who read simple sentences with confidence.

Ready for Chapters **Grades 2–4**
• chapters • longer paragraphs • full-color art
For children who want to take the plunge into chapter books but still like colorful pictures.

STEP INTO READING® is designed to give every child a successful reading experience. The grade levels are only guides; children will progress through the steps at their own speed, developing confidence in their reading.

Remember, a lifetime love of reading starts with a single step!

 Published in the United States by Random House Children's Books, a division of Penguin Random House LLC, 1745 Broadway, New York, NY 10019, and in Canada by Penguin Random House Canada Limited, Toronto.

Visit us on the Web!
StepIntoReading.com
rhcbooks.com

Educators and librarians, for a variety of teaching tools, visit us at
RHTeachersLibrarians.com

ISBN 978-1-9848-9445-8 (trade) — ISBN 978-1-9848-9446-5 (lib. bdg.)

Printed in the United States of America

10 9 8 7 6 5 4 3 2 1

STEP 1
READY TO READ
STEP INTO READING®
nick jr.

The Bean Team

by Tex Huntley

illustrated by Francesco Legramandi
and Gabriella Matta

Random House New York

Butterbean is
a fairy.

She loves

to cook.

She cooks
at her own café!

Poppy, Dazzle, and Jasper are Butterbean's friends.

They work

at the café, too.

Cricket is Butterbean's
little sister.

She loves to help!

Jasper delivers food
to the café.

He brings eggs,
milk, and butter.

Time to make cookies!

Mix, mix, mix.

Stir, stir, stir.

The cookies
are done!

Cricket adds
the frosting.

Butterbean adds
a fairy finish
with a magical bean.

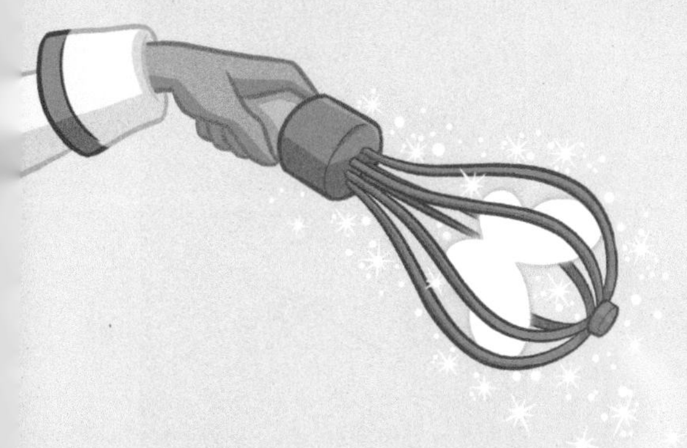

The bean's magic
makes the cookies fly.
They fly out the door!

Everyone follows
the cookies
back to the café.

They eat the cookies together!

Hooray for the team
at Butterbean's Café!